SCHOOL'S OUT

By Johanna Hurwitz

Johanna Hurwitz

SCHOOL'S OUT

ILLUSTRATED BY

SHEILA HAMANAKA

MORROW JUNIOR BOOKS
NEW YORK

1   2   3   4   5   6   7   8   9   10

Library of Congress Cataloging-in-Publication Data
Hurwitz, Johanna.
School's out / Johanna Hurwitz ; illustrated by Sheila Hamanaka.
p.   cm.
Summary: Lucas thinks his summer vacation is ruined when Mom hires
a French au pair to watch over Lucas and his two-year-old twin brothers.
ISBN 0-688-09938-6 (trade).
[1. Au pairs—Fiction.   2. Brothers—Fiction.]   I. Hamanaka,
Sheila, ill.   II. Title.
PZ7.H9574Sc   1990
[Fic]—dc20   90-13446 CIP AC

This book is for
Ellen & David Conford, good friends
(except for pages 9½–11,
which are dedicated to U.H.)

CONTENTS

SCHOOL'S OUT

· 1 ·
TWO SURPRISES

Lucas Cott had started out in third grade as the class clown. He constantly annoyed his teacher with silly behavior. He distracted his classmates from their work, and he didn't perform in class up to his ability. Gradually, though, as the third grade progressed, Lucas began to improve.

Now, on the last day of school, as Lucas ran home, he clutched three items in his hands. In addition to his report card, his teacher, Mrs. Hockaday, had given him a small package with three pencils. One of them was half red and half blue. If Lucas sharpened it at both ends, he could write in two colors. Mrs. Hockaday had given the same gift to every child in the class.

The proof of the *new* Lucas was the note on pink stationery that his teacher asked him to give his parents. The note was not meant for Lucas. However, as soon as he was outside the school building, he opened and read it, anyhow. It said "Lucas is no longer the rambunctious student he once was." Even though he did not know the meaning of the word *rambunctious*, Lucas was quite certain that the note was a good one. Hadn't Mrs. Hockaday smiled when she gave it to him?

Lucas was very eager to show the pencils and the note to his mother. He knew she would be proud of him. He was glad that this last day of school was only a half day. As soon as he ate his lunch, he could begin having a wonderful summer vacation.

Lucas was right. His mother was delighted with his report card. She beamed as she studied it and as she read the note from Mrs. Hockaday.

Marcus and Marius, Lucas's twin brothers, were happy, too. Even though they were not yet three years old, they loved to play with their big brother. They were surprised to see Lucas home at lunchtime. Most days, he went off in the morning and didn't return to their house until the middle of the afternoon.

"Lucas. Lucas!" Marius squealed with glee.

"Let's play," shouted Marcus, jumping up and down.

Mrs. Cott admired Lucas's gift from Mrs. Hockaday. "I have two surprises for you, too," she said. She went to the closet and returned with a large box wrapped in fancy paper.

"Yippee," shouted Lucas. He had not been expecting a gift from his mother. "It looks like a birthday present," he said.

"How can it be a birthday present?" Mrs. Cott laughed. "Your birthday was in February. This is a gift because your father and I are so proud of your improvement at school this year."

Lucas quickly ripped the paper from the package. He could not believe how many good things were happening in one day. It had never occurred to him that both his parents and his teacher would give him presents today.

He opened the box and pulled out something he really wanted. It was a blue-and-white plastic helmet to wear when he rode his bike.

"Oh, wow!" Lucas said. He'd been wanting a helmet all spring. He put the helmet on his head and fastened the chin strap. He could hardly wait to go off on his bike. He would look just as if he was riding a motorcycle.

"There's another surprise, too," said his mother.

Lucas looked around, expecting to see another package. All he saw were his brothers playing with the torn papers and the empty box from his helmet.

"Where is it?" he asked.

"The other surprise is something that hasn't arrived yet. It doesn't come in a box. Actually, it's a person. . . ."

Lucas stared at his mother in disbelief. This

was the way she had announced the forthcoming birth of his new baby sister or brother a few years ago. They were all surprised when the new baby turned out to be *two* babies.

"Do you mean that we're going to have another baby?" he asked her.

"Oh, no. My goodness, no!" Mrs. Cott laughed. "This is going to be a grown-up person. She's coming to spend the summer with us. Her name is Genevieve Lamont. She's from France and she'll help take care of you and Marcus and Marius."

Lucas thought his mother must be joking. School was over and he was supposed to be free. Now suddenly, a grown-up person was coming to his house. It would be like having a teacher living right inside the house with them all summer long. It would be like school all over again—only worse.

"Why does she have to come here?" he asked. "I don't need anyone to watch me."

"She is going to work as an au pair," Mrs. Cott explained.

"Oh pear?" asked Lucas. "What does that mean?"

"It's a French term. It's what they call a person who works for a family by taking care of their children and helping around the house. Genevieve will be here all summer. I'm sure you will like her. And it will mean that I have a bit of vacation, too. Marcus and Marius need a lot of attention."

"But you have me to help take care of them during the summer," Lucas protested.

"You'll help Genevieve take care of the twins. And you can help her with her English. One of the reasons she is coming here is to improve her command of our language."

Lucas looked down at his brothers. Marcus was tearing the wrapping paper from Lucas's gift into small pieces and chewing them.

"Marcus, spit that out at once," said his mother. She held her son's mouth open and the soggy paper fell out into her hand.

"You see? These boys need constant attention," Mrs. Cott said to Lucas.

"Did you ever wonder what it would be like if I had been twins, too?" asked Lucas.

"Impossible," said his mother, shuddering. "You are one of a kind . . . the one and only Lucas Cott. Thank goodness for that," she added.

"Let's play," shouted Marius. He was standing inside the box that had held the helmet.

"Let's eat lunch," said their mother. "There will be plenty of time for playing later." Mrs. Cott turned to her older son. "They don't remember last summer, so they don't understand that you are going to be home every day for more than two months."

Lucas frowned. With this strange "oh pear" person, he was no longer certain that he wanted to be home every day for over two months.

"When does the oh pear get here?" he asked.

"Not for another week," his mother said as she placed the food out on the kitchen table.

That was good. At least Lucas would have a few days to himself. "Ah." He sighed. "No homework, no studying, no rules . . ."

"Of course there are rules," said his mother.

"Every family has rules. For example, please go wash your hands before you eat. That's a rule."

"Home rules aren't as bad as school rules," said Lucas. He took off his helmet and then he went to the kitchen sink.

Marcus and Marius sat on their booster seats, and Lucas and his mother sat on either side of them. They had tuna-fish sandwiches. As a treat, Mrs. Cott made chocolate milk for all three boys. The twins drank their milk out of special mugs with only a small opening on the top. That was good because when Marius accidentally knocked his mug onto the floor, only a small amount of chocolate milk spilled out.

Lucas reached automatically and grabbed Marcus's mug. He knew his brothers well enough to know that when one twin did something accidentally, the other usually did it, too—on purpose.

"All done. Let's play," said Marcus. He pushed his plate away.

"Soon," said Mrs. Cott. "First, you fellows have to take your nap."

"No nap. No nap," protested Marius and Marcus together.

"Just a short one," their mother promised. "Then you can play with Lucas for a l-o-n-g time."

She helped the boys down from their seats and took them off into their bedroom.

Lucas got up from the table and put on his helmet again. "I'm going to ride my bike over to Julio's," he called to his mother. He wanted to show his friend his surprise gift. He also wanted some time to think about the other surprise. The best surprises come in gift-wrapped boxes, he decided. Other surprises usually stink.

· 2 ·
THE "OH PEAR" POPS CORN

During the days before her arrival, Lucas learned a bit more about Genevieve Lamont. She was eighteen years old and about to begin university classes in France in the fall.

"That's like college here," explained Mrs. Cott.

Genevieve's parents were friends of some people that Lucas's parents knew. Mr. and Mrs. Cott had heard that the young French woman was looking for a summer job in the United States.

"We offered her the possibility of staying here with us," said Lucas's mother.

Mr. and Mrs. Cott were busy making arrangements for Genevieve's stay. There was a room in the attic that had been used for storing suitcases and old furniture. Now it had been transformed into a bedroom for Genevieve.

"Will she be able to understand us?" Lucas was worried.

The only French words he knew were from the song *"Frère Jacques."* He had learned that when he was in first grade. He still remembered the words to the song, but he had forgotten what they all meant.

"Frère Jacques, Frère Jacques. Dormez-vous?"

"Will we eat a lot of French fries and French toast this summer?" he asked. He wouldn't complain about that.

"Neither of those is a French food," said his mother.

That didn't make any sense to Lucas at all.

When Lucas went to visit his friend Julio, he

discussed the expected arrival of Genevieve Lamont.

"Maybe you'll like her," said Julio hopefully.

Lucas had his doubts. "Why can't she go some-
place else to practice her English?" he asked.

"It's not easy to teach someone how to speak
in English," Julio warned him. "I've been working on my grandmother for years. She still hasn't
learned very much."

"Maybe you're not so hot as a teacher," said
Lucas. He wasn't sure he would be so hot, either.
Besides, who wanted to spend the summer teach-
ing someone how to speak English?

Julio shrugged his shoulders. "My grandmother is never going to bother speaking English
when she can talk to my mother and brothers in
Spanish," he said.

"My mother studied French at college, but she
says she has forgotten it all," said Lucas. "So
Genevieve won't be able to speak French to anyone at our house."

"If she is going to take care of your brothers,

she only needs to know one word," said Julio. He had seen Marcus and Marius at least a hundred times when he played at Lucas's house. "All she needs to know when she talks to them is the word NO."

When the day came for Genevieve to arrive, Mr. Cott thought they should all go to the airport to pick her up. However, his wife said that it might overwhelm the young girl.

"If Marcus and Marius get restless in the car, Genevieve may decide to get right back on a plane and go home," Lucas's mother said.

That sounded fine to Lucas.

So it was decided that only Lucas and his father would pick up the French visitor. Since neither of them knew what she looked like, Mr. Cott asked Lucas to make a sign saying WELCOME, GENE-VIEVE. Lucas's mother told him how to spell the French name. He hadn't known that it began with a G because it sounded like a J. Lucas wasn't sure he wanted to welcome Genevieve, but at least it gave him a chance to use his new red-and-blue pencil.

A tall young woman with long dark hair stopped when she saw Lucas's sign. "Allo," she said. "It is me. I am Genevieve."

Lucas was filled with relief. Here was the woman they had come to meet, and she knew how to speak English. Her way of speaking was a bit strange. She pronounced everything in a weird way, but at least he could understand her and he wouldn't have to bother doing any teaching.

"That's her French accent," Mr. Cott explained to Lucas afterward. Lucas's father also explained about the word *oui*, which Genevieve used in response to most things that were told to her. It was the way French people said yes. Although it sounded like *wee*, it was spelled *oui*.

Genevieve also said funny things, such as "We will have good times together. No?"

That certainly sounded like no, but Lucas realized she meant yes.

To Lucas, she said, "You will like me. No?"

No. He couldn't decide if he would like her or not.

It was strange to have Genevieve staying in the house. It wasn't the same as having his aunt or his grandmother come for a visit. The good thing, of course, was that he wasn't expected to kiss her at all. The bad thing was that although she brought presents when she came, they weren't things he liked. Genevieve brought a bottle of perfume to Mrs. Cott and a jar of French honey to Mr. Cott. The twins each received a little wooden car. Lucas received a book. It had loads of pictures, like a comic book, and was about someone named Tintin. All the words, though, were in French. What good was that?

"I will read it to you," Genevieve offered.

There was no way Lucas wanted Genevieve to read to him as if he were a baby.

The first evening, Mrs. Cott treated her like company.

"Would you like some more mashed potatoes? Did you have enough meat?"

Genevieve was fascinated by the twins. They were identical, and so, like everyone else meeting them for the first time, she couldn't tell them apart.

"How do you know which is Marcus and which is Marius?" she asked, turning to Lucas for help.

"It's a piece of cake," said Lucas.

"A piece of cake?" said Genevieve, looking confused. There were meat and potatoes and broccoli and salad on the table. There was no cake anywhere in sight.

"That's an English expression," said Mr. Cott, coming to Genevieve's aid. "Lucas means that for him, it is easy."

"A piece of cake," Genevieve repeated again. "Please excuse me," she said, and she got up quickly from the table.

Mr. and Mrs. Cott and Lucas looked at one another with puzzled expressions on their faces. Where had Genevieve gone?

A minute later, Genevieve returned carrying a small notebook and a pencil. "This was a present from my sister. I am going to write down in here the new words I learn." She opened the notebook and wrote the term *a piece of cake*.

"I will be very smart when I go home," she said.

The next morning, no longer wearing a fancy dress but, rather, jeans and a T-shirt like any American her age, Genevieve was kept busy wiping up the orange juice that Marcus knocked over onto the kitchen floor.

"Marius, you must be more careful. No?" she said.

"No. That's Marcus," Lucas corrected her.

"Marius needs to be more careful, too," commented Mrs. Cott. Marius had already dropped some of his scrambled eggs.

After breakfast, Lucas escaped to his swimming lesson at the local pool. He was already a good swimmer. Now he was learning how to dive.

When Lucas got home, he found Genevieve watching the twins as they rode their tricycles on the sidewalk in front of the house.

"Hello, Lucas," she called to him. To Lucas, it sounded more like "Allo, Lu'kas."

"Allo," he imitated her. He ran into the house to drop his bathing suit and damp towel into the laundry hamper.

That afternoon, Mrs. Cott went off to meet her husband. They had an invitation to dinner with some friends. "Genevieve is in charge," said Mrs. Cott. "There are many things about our house she still doesn't know, so I'm counting on you to help her out."

"I will be the general," said Genevieve. "Lucas will be my lieutenant." She smiled at her joke.

Lucas wondered if she was going to ask him to salute her.

"Genevieve is going to prepare supper," said Mrs. Cott as she got into the car.

"Au revoir," Genevieve called.

"Mommy," wailed Marcus.

"I'll be back soon," said Mrs. Cott.

"Mommy," wailed Marius.

The car pulled away, and Genevieve and Lucas were left with two crying boys.

"Mama will return," said Genevieve as she sat

down on the front step of the house and tried to put her arms around the boys.

Marius pulled away from her and began to jump up and down as he cried.

"Come, we will play a game together," said Genevieve, trying to get the attention of the crying children.

Lucas wondered how long it would take her to get them quiet. They would not play ball with her, and they refused to get on their bikes or to go on the swings in the yard. Genevieve began to look around for another distraction. Lucas decided to help her out.

"Let's make popcorn," he said in a loud voice.

Like magic, the twins both stopped crying.

"Do you make your own popcorn?" asked Genevieve. "At home, I buy the popcorn when I go to the cinema. I never made it myself."

"It's easy," said Lucas. "I'll show you."

He led the way inside. Marcus and Marius pushed to enter behind him. They both loved popcorn.

Lucas showed Genevieve the box of corn in

the cupboard. "You put a tiny bit of oil in a big pot," he told her. "Then when it gets hot, you add the corn and it pops. It only takes a few seconds."

Genevieve shook the unpopped corn in the box. "This is a very American thing," she said.

Lucas found a deep pot for Genevieve. He let her pour the cooking oil into the pot and turn on the stove. He wasn't allowed to do that himself.

"In a minute, you put one piece of corn into the pot," he instructed her. "When it pops, you know the oil is hot enough to put in the rest of the corn."

Marcus and Marius stood in silence. They were waiting for the popcorn. Genevieve put a single kernel into the pot. After a minute, they heard a faint hiss and then the sound of the little yellow kernel exploding into a beautiful white piece.

"Now put the rest of the corn into the pot," said Lucas.

He was just about to tell Genevieve to put the

lid on the pot when something stopped him. He had always wondered what would happen if you didn't put a lid on the pot. It would be much more fun to watch the kernels as they exploded into white pieces.

"Shake the pot a little," said Lucas. He liked telling General Genevieve what to do.

"Popcorn. I want popcorn," said Marcus, bursting with anticipation.

"Soon. Very soon," Lucas promised.

They heard a pop and then another.

"See? It's almost ready," he told his brothers.

Then all at once, the popping started in earnest. There was a constant *pop-pop-pop* sound as all the kernels in the pot reached the right temperature for popping. Suddenly, Lucas discovered why the instructions always said to cover the pot.

Popcorn began to fly out of the pot and onto the floor.

"Popcorn!" shrieked Marcus with glee.

"Popcorn!" shouted Marius as he gathered up

pieces from the floor and put them inside his mouth.

Both twins sat down on the floor and scooped up the white pieces.

"Good!" said Marcus.

"Good popcorn!" said Marius.

Genevieve turned off the stove. She found a large bowl in the cupboard and poured the popcorn that remained inside the pot into it. Then she studied the box in which the corn had been stored.

"Lucas," she said, "you forgot to tell me something very important. No?"

Once again, her no meant yes.

"No," said Lucas, looking at her with wide-eyed innocence.

"In America, do you always cook the popcorn so it falls on the floor?" she asked him.

"Sure," said Lucas. "The floor is clean. And it's a good game for Marcus and Marius." The latter had crawled under the kitchen table to get a couple of pieces that had landed there.

"They're not crying anymore," he pointed out.

"That is true," said Genevieve. She smiled at Lucas. "It is good I washed the kitchen floor this afternoon for your mother." She pushed the bowl toward Lucas. "Have a piece!" she offered.

Lucas reached his hand toward the bowl. Before he could get at it, though, Genevieve lifted the bowl above his head. Then she tipped it over. The corn rained over Lucas's head and onto the kitchen floor.

Genevieve sat down on the floor. "Come, Lucas," she invited him. "We will all eat the popcorn on the floor. It is the new American way that I learned today. No?"

"Yes," said Lucas, but he meant no.

He sat down on the floor and began to eat the popcorn.

· 3 ·
WHICH IS WHICH?

A few days after Genevieve Lamont arrived, Julio rode his bike over to Lucas's house. The twins were playing on the swing set in the backyard, and Lucas was watching them. It was Genevieve's day off.

"I want you to teach me which is which," said Julio.

"What do you mean *which is which*?" asked Lucas.

"Your brothers. They look the same to me.

But you always know which is which. What's the trick?"

"It's not a trick," said Lucas. "I've been trying to show Genevieve the same thing. Look. You can tell by their freckles. He took Julio over to see. Lucas stopped the swing and asked Marcus to get off for a minute. Then he pointed to the back of his brother's chubby leg. "Look, Julio. See? Marcus has a freckle on the back of his knee. Even though they are identical, Marius doesn't have a freckle there."

"Hey, that's great," said Julio, smiling. He thought for a minute. Then he said, "But how can you tell them apart when they are wearing long pants? Now it's summer, so they have shorts on. But in the winter you know which is which, too. You can't see the freckle on his knee then."

"Easy," said Lucas. He helped Marcus back onto the swing and gave him a push. "Marius has a freckle, too. It's behind his ear."

Julio nodded his head. "Okay," he said. "I can remember that." He thought again. "What happens if he gets dirty?"

"What do you mean?" asked Lucas. "He always gets dirty."

"If your brother gets dirty, you can't see the freckle behind his ear."

"It doesn't matter," said Lucas, shrugging his shoulders. "I can tell them apart without looking at the freckles."

"But how?"

"I don't know," said Lucas. "I just know them. After all, they *are* my brothers."

"It's weird that they are so much alike," said Julio, studying the twins closely. "What do you think it feels like?"

"I don't know," said Lucas. He had often wondered about it himself. How would it be to have a brother who was just his age and looked just like him? Would the brother do everything he did? When he woke up in the morning, would he ever be confused about who he was and who his brother was?

"I have an idea," said Julio. "Let's see if we can find other ways that they are different . . . besides freckles."

"Like what?" asked Lucas.

Julio thought for a minute. "Which of you guys can jump up and down the longest?" he asked the twins. He started jumping up and down to demonstrate.

Marcus and Marius both got off the swings and began jumping. They thought it was a new game. Lucas and Julio watched until one of the twins stopped.

"Okay. You're the winner," said Julio. He looked behind the knees of both boys. "Marcus wins," he said. "He jumped the longest."

"You got confused," said Lucas. "It was Marius who jumped the longest. Marcus has the freckle, but Marius jumped longer."

Julio was not discouraged. "We should write this all down. That way, we won't forget. Could you get a piece of paper? I'll think of another contest," he said.

Lucas went inside the house and returned with a pad of paper and a newly sharpened pencil. It was one of his prize pencils from Mrs. Hockaday.

"How about running? Which twin runs the fastest?" asked Julio.

They lined up Marcus and Marius. "When I say to run, you both should run to the fence," said Lucas. He pointed to the wooden fence that divided their property from their neighbors'. "Then turn around and come back to me. Okay?"

Marcus and Marius nodded. They liked all these new games.

"One-two-three-go," shouted Julio.

The twins stood looking at him.

"Why aren't you running?" asked Lucas.

"You didn't say it," said Marius.

Lucas grinned. "I taught them how to play Simon Says. I guess they think this is a game called Lucas Says." He turned to his brothers. "Okay. Run."

The twins started off. Marius tripped on a tree root and fell.

"I got a boo-boo," he said. He went over to Lucas so that his big brother could rub the spot.

"We'll have to do it over," said Julio.

By the end of the afternoon, they had made a whole chart.

Longest jumper	Marcus
Fastest runner	Marius
Eats most cookies	Marius
Gets dirtiest	tie
Hops longest on one foot	Marcus
Longest clapper	tie
Loudest voice	tie

"If I study this like I study things for school, then I'll know all about your brothers," said Julio. "Probably by the next time I come to play with you, I'll be able to tell them apart, just like you."

"Naw," said Lucas. "You'll have to ask them to jump or hop or something. I know who they are when they are standing still or sleeping or anything."

"When they're sleeping, it doesn't matter which is which," Julio declared.

"I wonder if Genevieve will be able to tell them apart by the end of the summer," said Lucas.

"I better leave this chart for her," Julio said as he got ready to go home. "She has a real tough job."

"Which boy is the most trouble?" Lucas asked his parents the next evening. "Marcus or Marius?" It would be another thing to add to Julio's list.

"They both know how to horse around equally well," said Mr. Cott.

"Horse? How can they be a horse?" asked Genevieve. "They don't walk on their hands and feet."

This was another example of how, even though she seemed to understand English so well, some expressions were new to her.

"I mean that they are both wild and noisy," Mr. Cott explained.

Genevieve removed the little notebook from the pocket of her jeans. Hardly a day passed when she didn't learn a new word or phrase. Yesterday Lucas had taught her *fat chance* and about *acting chicken*.

"Was I as bad as Marcus and Marius when I was little?" Lucas asked.

Today had been a particularly trying day for Genevieve. The twins had been playing happily in the plastic wading pool in the backyard one minute. The next moment, Marcus had climbed out of the pool and taken off his little swimming trunks.

"While Genevieve was putting the trunks back on Marcus, Marius climbed out of the pool and took off *his* trunks," Mrs. Cott related to her husband. "And then he ran down the street with nothing on. Genevieve found him all the way down at the corner."

"It is good that he knows he must not cross the street," said Genevieve. "Otherwise, he would have gone even farther."

"Did I do things like that when I was little?" asked Lucas. He couldn't remember being two years old.

"You never took off your clothes and ran down the street," said Mrs. Cott. "But I'll never forget the incident with the little men."

"Who are the little men?" asked Lucas.

"You were a bit older than Marcus and Marius. I guess you must have been four years old. You had just gotten a new pair of scissors and you liked cutting with them. I gave you an old magazine, and you cut out pictures of cars and babies and things like that. The next thing I knew, you had gone to my pocketbook and taken out my money. I found you sitting on the floor busily cutting out the little men."

"What little men?" asked Genevieve.

"The little men on the money," said his mother. "Lucas didn't know their names at the time. One little man was George Washington. The other little man was Abraham Lincoln."

"Could you still spend the money?" asked Lucas. It was funny to think that once he had been just as bad as Marcus and Marius. In fact, it sounded to him as if he had been as naughty as his two brothers together, even though he was the one and only kid in the family at the time.

"I took all the pieces to the bank, and they let me exchange the money. The teller at the bank suggested that I take all my money in quarters because you wouldn't be able to destroy them."

"Did you?" asked Lucas.

"No," said Mrs. Cott. "That many coins would have been too heavy. So I took home dollar bills and learned to be more careful around you."

"Now you have to be more careful with Marcus and Marius," said Lucas.

4
WET PAINT

One of the plans that Lucas's parents had for the summer was to get the outside of the house painted. When Lucas first heard about the project, he was very excited. He thought that he would be able to help. He liked the idea of climbing to the top of a tall ladder and applying a fresh coat of white paint to the sides of the house.

"Don't be silly, Lucas," said his mother. "This is a major undertaking. We've hired a professional painting company. There are a couple of men coming to do the job for us."

"Well, at least I can watch," said Lucas.

"You can watch, but keep away from the paint," said Mrs. Cott. She turned to face the twins as she spoke so they would know she meant them, too. "I don't want to find any paint on your clothes," she said. "Remember, the paint is to go on the house and not on you."

The painters were supposed to come the first Monday in July, but they were behind schedule. So it was the middle of the month when the van and the two painters finally arrived to paint the Cott house.

Lucas stood outside the house with Marcus and Marius and Genevieve. They all watched as the men set up their ladders. They put huge drop cloths on the ground around the house. It was like watching a TV show. The men didn't begin to paint at once. First, they climbed the ladders and scraped at bits of flaking paint. They removed the shutters from all the windows.

"The man is breaking the house," said Marius.

He seemed to be marveling that someone could do something that seemed so naughty.

"He's not breaking the house," Genevieve explained. "He must take down the shutters so he can paint underneath them. Your mother said that the shutters will be painted red."

"I like red," said Marcus, nodding his head with approval.

"Remember to like it but not touch it," said Mrs. Cott, coming out of the house. "Don't forget what I said. I don't want any paint on your clothes. Keep your fingers out of the paint cans." She turned to look at each of the twins. "Do you understand?" she said. "Not one single drop of paint on your hands."

"No paint on my hands," Marcus promised.

"No paint on my hands," said Marius. He looked down at the navy shorts and navy-and-red striped T-shirt he was wearing. "No paint," he said again.

After lunch, Lucas got on his bike and went to meet some boys in the local park, where they were going to play ball. By the time he returned home, the painters had begun the actual job of painting. They worked with large rollers that they dipped into the cans of white paint.

Genevieve had moved the plastic wading pool from its usual place near the side of the house. Now it was located farther away from the house and from the painters. Marcus and Marius were just getting out of the water.

Marius ran over to Lucas. "Look at the house," he said, pointing to the newly painted section.

Lucas nodded his head.

"Lucas, please watch your brothers for a minute. I forgot to bring towels," called Genevieve. She turned and went inside the house.

Marcus came running over to Lucas now, too. "Look at all the paint," he said, pulling his big brother by the hand toward the nearest open can.

Lucas looked into the can. The white paint had a shiny appearance inside the can that it didn't have once it was applied to the sides of the house. It looked cool and inviting, like a vat of milk or, even better, melted marshmallows.

"Paint looks good," said Marcus.

Lucas grinned at his brother. "Yep," he agreed, nodding his head. It looked good to him, too.

Marcus stood right next to the paint pail. Lucas knew he should pull him away from it, but he didn't. It wasn't his job. Genevieve had come all the way from France to watch the twins. It was her job to see that they didn't go near the paint.

Lucas wondered if his brother would dare to put his hand in the pail. He stood watching to see what Marcus would do.

Marcus didn't put his hand in the pail. He lifted his foot and stuck it right inside the can.

"Marcus!" shouted Lucas. It was hard to believe his brother had really done that. He grabbed the little boy, and the white paint dripped off his foot and onto the lawn.

"Me, too," screamed Marius, and he ran toward the can of paint.

"No, no," shouted Lucas. He dropped Marcus on the grass and ran to get Marius. He knew his mother was going to be furious, but he couldn't help laughing. Marcus had what looked like a white sock on his foot. All around, the grass was marked with bits of white paint, too. At least he had prevented Marius from getting a matching sock on his foot.

"Lucas. What did you do?" exclaimed Genevieve as she emerged from the house carrying a couple of towels.

"Me?" said Lucas. "I didn't do anything. He did it. Not me."

"I told you to watch them for one minute and look what happened," Genevieve said. She approached Marcus cautiously. She didn't want to get a drop of that paint on her.

Marius was squirming in Lucas's grasp. Lucas put his brother down on the ground. "It's not my fault," Lucas protested, though he knew very well he could have prevented Marcus's action.

"Yes it is," said Genevieve. "You know these boys. One must never take one's eyes off them, not for a second. Your mother will be furious with me. But it's not my fault. It's your fault."

"It would have happened if I hadn't been here," Lucas asserted. He remembered how

tempting the white paint had looked to him. No wonder Marcus had not been able to resist the urge to stick his foot inside.

One of the painters climbed down from the ladder. "Hey, kid," he shouted.

Lucas and Genevieve looked at the painter. Then their eyes went to the spot where the painter was pointing. There was Marius standing with not one but two feet inside the can of paint.

"Cold," said Marius when he saw everyone looking at him. "Cold paint."

"Wet," shouted Genevieve. "That's wet paint."

"Cold and wet," said Marius, nodding his head.

"If you leave the paint on, you'll know which is which,"suggested Lucas. He started laughing again. "Marius has two white socks. Marcus has one." He thought it was a great joke. Probably Julio would appreciate it, too.

Genevieve did not think it was funny. "I am surprised at you, Lucas Cott," she said in an angry voice.

Lucas couldn't understand why all her anger was directed at him and not at the twins. They had been naughty, not him. However, as he watched her removing the paint, he started thinking. He remembered how he had insisted to his mother that he was able to take care of Marcus and Marius and that they didn't need any outside help from an au pair girl. This afternoon, though, he hadn't helped with the twins at all. He had let them get paint on themselves when he could have prevented it.

It took a whole hour for Genevieve to remove the "white socks" from the feet and ankles of both twins.

When Mrs. Cott returned home from shopping, there were still some traces of the paint remaining on the boys. "I am so sorry," said Genevieve. Lucas was relieved that she didn't mention that he had been watching the twins when they got the paint on them.

"Didn't I tell you not to get any paint on you?" Mrs. Cott asked Marcus and Marius.

"No paint on my clothes," said Marius proudly.

Marcus waved his fingers in front of his mother's face. "No paint on my hands," he said.

Mrs. Cott nodded her head slowly. "I guess it's my fault," she said. "I never told them not to stick their feet into the paint cans."

Lucas knew it was his fault, too.

· 5 · LUCAS ON THE ROOF

The two painters worked at Lucas's house for several days. Each morning, Lucas watched them with envy. It looked like so much fun to climb the steep ladders that were propped against the house. Applying the fresh white paint looked like fun, too. Maybe he would get a job as a housepainter when he grew up.

On the third day that the painters were working at the Cott house, Lucas was home alone. Lucas's father was off at work. His mother had gone off in the car with the twins and Genevieve. Today was the day that Marcus and Marius were scheduled for a checkup and booster shots at the pediatrician's. Lucas was watching the painters and waiting for Julio.

Lucas walked around the house, admiring the painters' work. Three sides of the house were freshly painted. At the rate the men were working, this might be their last day. Lucas wished that he had climbed to the top of one of the huge ladders. He should have done it yesterday evening when the men had gone home and his family was in the house. Now no one in his family was around to scold, but the men were busy painting. He knew if he tried to climb on one of the ladders now, he would be ordered to get off.

He stood admiring the ladder leaning against the front of the house. It reached right up to the roof. One of the painters was standing on the roof at this very moment. Lucas thought it would be great fun to climb the ladder and sit up there. Then he would be able to see all over town. He would see people doing their errands, walking their dogs, and mowing their lawns. He would be able to see Julio as he rode his bike toward Lucas's house.

Lucas walked over to the ladder to examine it. The ladder was stained with dried bits of every color of paint that the men had ever used. Lucas reached out and touched the ladder with his hands. It felt good and steady. He raised his right foot and placed it on the first rung of the ladder. Before he had time to put all his weight on his right foot and lift his left foot up, he felt the ladder begin to move slightly.

Lucas put his foot back on the ground and looked up.

The painter who had been standing on the roof was coming down. Since he came down backward, though, he didn't notice Lucas standing at the bottom. Lucas quickly moved farther away from the ladder.

"Listen," the painter said, "we have to go off for a little while. There's a lady a couple of blocks away who wants us to look at her house and give an estimate."

Lucas looked at the painter. He was wearing a hat, but bits of red hair stuck out. The hair, the hat, and even his face were spattered with tiny specks of white paint. What fun to get paint on you and not have anyone scold, Lucas thought.

The second painter came down from another ladder at the side of the house. Lucas looked from one painter to the other and grinned. The second man had a streak of white paint along the side of his nose.

"Keep away from the paint," said the red-haired painter. "We don't want any of it to spill."

"I won't touch the paint," Lucas promised solemnly. "Cross my heart and hope to die," he added, hoping to convince the men of his sincerity. After all, they had seen what his brothers had done with the paint two days ago.

"Good," said the painter.

The men got into their pickup truck and drove off. Lucas watched the truck disappear down the street. Then he turned back toward the house. He could hardly believe his good luck. He had no intention of touching the paint, but no one had said anything about touching the ladders. This would be his chance!

Lucas walked over to the ladder that reached the roof. He put his hands along the sides of the ladder. He lifted his right foot and hoisted himself onto the first rung. The ladder shook slightly from his weight. He raised his left foot. There was a bigger distance between rungs than he had realized, but he was able to manage. He put his right foot up, then his left foot up. The slight motion of the ladder was a bit scary, but he kept on going. When he was midway up the ladder, he turned his head around. When he looked down, he felt dizzy. He held on to the sides of the ladder more tightly than before. He was really very high. He was already higher than the top of the jungle gym in the playground. He was higher than his bedroom window. Maybe this was high enough and he should go back down.

"Lucas Cott! What are you doing?" a voice called up to him.

Lucas froze on the ladder. Without turning

around, he recognized the voice. It was Cricket Kaufman, who had been in his class at school. What was she doing spying on him in his own yard?

"Does your mother know what you are doing?" Cricket shouted up at him.

"My mother isn't home. Besides, it's none of your business. What are you doing here?" Lucas shouted back. The problem was that he couldn't really turn around and face her because he was still feeling a bit dizzy from the last time he had looked down. Instead, he held the sides of the ladder tightly and stood still for a minute. It was impossible to argue with someone when you had your back to them and you were many feet above their head.

"You better come down right away," said Cricket. "You could kill yourself."

Lucas had no intention of killing himself. He also had no intention of giving Cricket the satisfaction of getting him to do what she wanted. Lucas ignored Cricket Kaufman and continued climbing up the ladder. With each step he took, he could hear Cricket shouting.

"Lucas Cott. Stop. Come down," she cried.

Lucas reached the top of the ladder and stepped over it and onto the flat surface at the front of the roof. He looked down at Cricket and the ground below. He felt dizzy from the height, so he sat down. You couldn't fall down if you were sitting.

"What are you doing here?" Lucas called down to Cricket. At school, she often bugged him. Looking down at her from this height, Lucas felt much more important, though. Now that he was seated, he didn't feel dizzy anymore. Too bad he couldn't always speak with Cricket Kaufman from this angle.

"What are you doing up there?" Cricket shouted back.

"I live here. I can sit wherever I want. It's my house. Besides, I asked you first. What are *you* doing here?"

"I came to give this to your mother." Cricket

held up a book. "My mother is lending it to her. It's all about being a good parent."

"My mother doesn't need that book," Lucas shouted down to Cricket.

"Oh yeah? Then how come she asked my mother if she could borrow it?" demanded Cricket.

Lucas shrugged his shoulders. "My mother isn't home," he called to his classmate. "But you can leave that in the house on the kitchen table. The door is open."

Cricket went inside the house with the book.

A minute later, she was back outside again. "You better get down, Lucas," she shouted up at him. "I'm not going home until you climb down."

"Then you're going to have a long, long wait," Lucas called back. "Why don't you come up here?" he urged Cricket. "I can see your house and I can see the school and everything. It's great."

"Do you think I'm crazy like you? I wouldn't

climb up to a roof," shouted Cricket. "You could fall."

"I won't fall," said Lucas. "This part of the roof is flat. There's nothing to be scared of." Lucas grinned down at Cricket. "I dare you to climb up here, too."

"Darers go first," Cricket retorted automatically. The kids always said that at school. Suddenly, Cricket realized what she had said. It was too late to take the words back.

"I already did it," said Lucas. "Now it's your turn."

"Well, I don't care," said Cricket, "I'm not climbing up this ladder."

"You're chicken!" shouted Lucas. "Chicken. Chicken."

"I am not," said Cricket. "But I'm not crazy like you, either."

"Chicken. You're chicken," Lucas taunted his classmate.

It was too much for Cricket. "Stop that, Lucas. You'll see. I'm coming right up. Right now."

From where he was sitting, Lucas couldn't see Cricket as she mounted the ladder, but he could hear the sound of her steps as she began to climb.

"Hold tight," Lucas called in warning. He didn't want to be responsible for Cricket falling off the ladder. He could hear her steps getting closer. He could also hear Cricket talking to herself. "I think I can. I think I can," she said.

Lucas recognized the words. They were in a story about a little train that his father read aloud to Marcus and Marius. He had read the story to Lucas when he was little, too.

"I think I can. I think I can," said Cricket. Then suddenly and amazingly, Cricket's head appeared at the top of the ladder. She really had done it.

"I can't believe I did this," Cricket said as she climbed over the top of the ladder and walked cautiously on the roof toward Lucas. She sat down beside him. "It's scary, but it's a little bit fun, too," she admitted. "Wouldn't it be funny if we had our whole class up here?"

"Even Mrs. Hockaday?" asked Lucas. He tried

to imagine Mrs. Hockaday standing with her open-toed shoes up on his roof. It was a funny thought, but not much funnier than actually sitting on the roof next to Cricket Kaufman.

"Hey, Lucas!" a voice shouted up at him.

It was Julio. He was jumping up and down and waving up at Lucas. "Why did you climb up there with Cricket?" Julio's voice sounded a little angry. "I thought I was your best friend," he said.

"Cricket did it on a dare," said Lucas.

"I'm coming up, too," said Julio, not waiting for a dare or an invitation.

Lucas and Cricket heard Julio climbing up the ladder.

Julio made it up much more quickly than either Lucas or Cricket. First of all, he had longer legs. And he was the best athlete in their class.

"Man, this is neat," shouted Julio as he joined Lucas and Cricket. He sat down by his classmates on the rooftop. "We can see everything from here."

Julio turned his head about. "Look." He

pointed. "There's my street. And that's my house."

When Lucas looked across at the treetops or at the roofs of the nearby houses, he felt great. It was only when he looked down that he felt the dizziness return.

Lucas took a quick look down at the street. He thought he saw the pickup truck that belonged to the painters coming toward the house. What would they say to see him and his classmates up on the roof?

A car door slammed down below. The truck Lucas had seen was indeed the one that belonged to the painters. Both men came and stood at the foot of the ladder.

"What are you doing up there?" called one.

"Sitting and looking at you," said Lucas. Even if they made him go down now, at least he had had his chance to climb the ladder.

A second car door banged shut. "Lucas Cott! Get down from there at once!" a voice screamed.

"Lucas. Lucas." More voices shouted at him.

It was his mother and Genevieve and the twins.

Lucas waved to all of them. Even if he was in big trouble for what he had done, he was glad he had done it.

"Hello, Mrs. Cott," called Cricket.

"Is that Cricket Kaufman up there with you?" shouted Mrs. Cott incredulously.

"It's me," Cricket announced. "Lucas dared me, and I did it!"

"Well, get down at once, all of you," shouted Mrs. Cott. "What is your mother going to say, Cricket?"

"I don't know," said Cricket, giggling. "I never climbed up on a roof before."

"None of us did," said Lucas. "That's why we had to do it."

Lucas knew that going down the ladder would be harder than going up. You had to go backward.

"You go first," Lucas said to Cricket.

"I don't want to," said Cricket. A minute ago, she had been giggling, but now she looked as if she might cry.

"Ladies first," Lucas insisted.

"I'm not a lady," said Cricket. "I'm just a girl. And I'm afraid I'll fall."

"Naw, you won't fall," said Julio. "It's easy."

"Then you go first," said Cricket.

"Sure," said Julio. He stood up and walked over to the ladder. When he had his hands on the ladder, however, he couldn't seem to make his feet move at all. He stood looking down. "It's really high up here, isn't it?" he said.

"Lucas, what's taking you so long?" Mrs. Cott screamed.

Lucas knew that he should go down the ladder first and show his friends that it was easy, but he just sat and rubbed his hand against the rough surface of the roof. He had been so busy planning his climb up that he had never thought about climbing down.

Cricket started to cry. "It's all your fault, Lucas Cott. We'll have to stay up here forever."

At that moment, though, they could hear that someone was climbing up the ladder. For one second, Lucas thought it might be his mother. It wasn't. It was the red-haired painter.

"You crazy kids," said the painter as he reached the top of the ladder. He reached for Julio, who was standing at the ladder, and helped him turn around so his face looked toward the house and his feet could go down the rungs, backward.

"Take it slowly," said the painter. "I'm right behind you. You won't fall. Just go one step at a time. You can do it. I do it every day."

"But we're not painters!" Cricket sobbed. "I'm going to be a lawyer when I grow up. And lawyers don't climb ladders."

"You should have thought of that before," said the painter, but he smiled at Cricket. "I won't let you fall," he promised. So Cricket went down after Julio.

Then it was Lucas's turn. Lucas took one peek downward as he began his descent. His stomach churned and he thought he would throw up his whole breakfast. He squeezed his eyes shut and held as tightly as he could to the sides of the ladder.

"I think I can. I think I can," he told himself, and he lowered his right foot, trying to find the location of the rung below. When his foot landed safely on the rung, he felt a surge of relief.

"I think I can. I think I can," he repeated again, and he was still a bit closer to the bottom. It felt as if it took an hour to get all the way down.

When he reached the bottom, Julio and Cricket were waiting for him. Mrs. Cott, Genevieve, Marcus and Marius, and both the painters were standing at the foot of the ladder waiting, too. Lucas's mother looked as white as the white paint.

As punishment for doing something so reckless as climbing the ladder, his mother said Lucas had to spend the rest of the day inside the house. He couldn't go off to the swimming pool with Julio.

"See you tomorrow," Julio said as he got on his bike and departed without Lucas.

"See you in fourth grade," said Cricket as she started off toward home.

Lucas went inside. He was relieved to be down on the ground again, but he was still a tiny bit glad he had climbed the ladder. It was worth staying in the house for the rest of the day, he thought. He didn't tell that to his mother, though. "I promised the painters that I wouldn't touch the paint," he said. "No one said that I shouldn't climb up on their ladder to the roof."

"Some things don't need to be said," said Mrs. Cott. "You could have been killed, and Julio and Cricket with you."

That afternoon, the painters finished their job.

Lucas watched from the window as they packed up all their gear—the canvas drop sheets, the paint cans and brushes, the long rollers, and the ladders.

Without the tall ladders, he would never again be able to climb up to the roof, he thought. Neither Marcus nor Marius would be able to climb the ladder, either. He hadn't worried too much about Cricket or Julio, but it would have been awful if the twins had managed to get up onto the roof.

Nothing he or the twins had ever done had gotten his mother so upset as this. He wondered why being naughty was so tempting. After all, even Cricket had gone up on the roof!

· 6 ·
LUCAS VS. GENEVIEVE

After the roof-climbing incident, Mrs. Cott was afraid to let Lucas out of her sight.

"I knew I had to watch the twins every moment. I didn't know that I had to keep an eye on you at all times, too," she complained to Lucas.

"You don't have to watch me. I won't climb to the roof again." It was an easy promise to make now that the tall ladders were gone. In September, the painters were going to return to paint inside the house. Lucas would be back at school by then.

Lucas's father also scolded him about climbing up to the roof. "I expected more responsible behavior from you," he said to Lucas. "Genevieve came primarily to help out with the twins. Now I see that she has to watch after you, as well."

"Aw, Dad. I don't need a baby-sitter," Lucas complained. "I promise I won't get into any trouble." Despite his promises, Lucas seemed to have lost his parents' trust for the time being. They wouldn't let him accept an invitation to go to the beach with Julio and his older brothers. They wouldn't let him go to an amusement park with another of his friends from school. They wouldn't even permit him to ride his bike off the block. If he had known that there would be such a fuss, Lucas would certainly have thought twice before he climbed that ladder up to the roof.

For now, Mrs. Cott was keeping a cautious eye on Lucas. For the next few days, she insisted that he stay close to the house. Either she or Genevieve was watching him all the time. It also meant that Lucas had to go wherever they went.

When the au pair girl had first arrived, Mrs. Cott had discovered that Genevieve was a very competent driver. So now Lucas found himself forced to accompany Genevieve when she went off on errands for his mother. He went with her to pick up dry cleaning or to buy something at the hardware store. The worst thing was having to accompany Genevieve with the long shopping list to the supermarket.

There was nothing in the world more boring than going to the supermarket, Lucas decided. However, Genevieve beamed. "I love American markets," she explained to Lucas. "There is so much to see. There are so many things to choose. I could walk around this supermarket all day long."

So Lucas stood by her side as Genevieve chose string beans from a huge bin. He watched in agony as Genevieve carefully selected first one bean and then another, instead of grabbing a fistful at a time. At this rate, it would take a week just to get a pound of beans.

"What a terrible waste," said Genevieve. She pointed to a man who was cutting the leaves off the tops of the celery. "You can use those to make soup," she said. "In your country, there is too much waste," she complained to Lucas.

Next, Genevieve selected some fruit. As she was looking over the cherries, she picked them out of the bin, one at a time. If she was picking them off a tree, it wouldn't have taken so long.

Genevieve was horrified to see a store employee removing bruised peaches and throwing them into a rubbish can. "See," she said. "That is more waste. Those peaches could be cooked into a wonderful compote."

Lucas didn't know what a compote was, so he just shrugged his shoulders. Would they ever get through his mother's shopping list at this rate?

Lucas stood with his hands on the shopping cart, eager to move on. At least they didn't have the twins with them. He watched as mothers moved past them with toddlers sitting in the carts. The little kids were giving orders. "Buy this. Buy that."

He did know how those kids felt, however. Seeing all the shelves filled with food was making him hungry.

"Let's hurry up so we can go home for lunch," said Lucas. "I could eat a horse."

Genevieve looked at Lucas with surprise. "I heard that you do not eat horsemeat here in America," she said. "In France, we have special butcher shops that sell only horsemeat."

Lucas made a face. He guessed he wasn't that hungry, after all. He explained to Genevieve that eating a horse was just an expression. As always, she took out her notebook to write it down.

"You are a good teacher, Lucas," she said.

Finally, Genevieve was ready to move on. Lucas pushed the cart toward the aisle of cookies. "Graham crackers," she read from the list that Lucas's mother had given her. She studied all the other types of cookies displayed on the shelves.

Graham crackers were the most boring cookies in the world, Lucas thought. He looked with Genevieve at the chocolate and cream-filled cookies. Lucas's eyes landed on a package of chocolate-covered graham crackers.

"Here," he said. "These are the ones."

"Okay," said Genevieve, dropping the package into the cart.

As they moved on, Lucas felt he had had at least one victory. He knew his mother would never have purchased chocolate-covered graham crackers. Marcus and Marius would be covered in chocolate themselves before they finished chewing up their cookies.

Genevieve picked out a package of chicken parts at the meat counter. At the fish department, she selected some fillets of fish to cook for supper. Lucas made another face. He knew fish was on his mother's shopping list, but fish was one of his least favorite things to eat.

Genevieve studied all twenty-seven types of mustard that were displayed near the meat counter. She even studied all the varieties of dog and cat food, despite the fact that the Cott family didn't own either a dog or a cat.

"These sound delicious," she said, picking up

a can of tuna, shrimp, and crab all mixed together for the gourmet cat.

When they passed the ice-cream freezer, Lucas saw a notice that the store brand of ice cream was on special sale. A half-gallon of the store brand cost less than a pint of one of the other brands. Mrs. Cott's list had said ice cream.

"Hey, Jennie, buy this one," said Lucas, picking a container that seemed most appealing to him. It was marshmallow fudge. So a half-gallon of marshmallow fudge ripple went into the shopping cart. That was victory number two for Lucas.

"Why did you call me Jennie?" the French girl asked Lucas.

Lucas shrugged his shoulders. The name had just popped out of his mouth. "It's a good nickname for you," he said.

"Nickname?" said Genevieve. It was a new word for her notebook.

It took about forty minutes for them to wait on line. They had too many groceries to stand at the express checkout, which was for customers with ten items or less. The people ahead of them on line had carts piled high with hundreds of cans and boxes and packages. It looked like enough food to last a family for a whole year. Lucas was sure their turn would never come.

Genevieve didn't seem to mind waiting at all. She looked into the other shopping carts to see what these people bought. She started a discussion with the woman ahead of them about the difference in taste of fresh beans, frozen beans, and canned beans. Naturally, the woman noticed Genevieve's accent, and before long they were having a conversation about traveling in France. The woman opened her pocketbook and showed Genevieve pictures of her children, who were away at summer camp. Lucas saw that Genevieve and the woman would know each other's whole life story before it was time to pay for the groceries. This sure was a boring way to spend a morning. Lucas was so impatient that he felt as if he would explode.

Finally, it was their turn. The groceries were put on the counter, and the cashier tallied the cost. Everything was put in heavy paper bags, and Lucas put the bags back into the cart so he could take them to the car.

"At home, there are no paper bags," said Genevieve, fingering the sturdy brown paper bags.

"How can you carry your groceries?" Lucas asked. He tried to imagine walking out of the supermarket with all their purchases spilling out of his arms.

"Most people take baskets or string bags from home," said Genevieve. "We do not waste so much paper."

Lucas shrugged. "We don't have any baskets at my house," he reminded the au pair girl.

When all the bags were in the trunk of the car, they drove off home. Lucas was relieved that this chore was finished at last. When he got to the house, though, he had to help Genevieve take all the bags into the house. Then his mother made him help put the groceries away in the kitchen cupboards and in the refrigerator.

"Oh dear!" Mrs. Cott sighed as she looked over their purchases. "I should have explained to Genevieve about getting *plain* graham crackers."

Lucas pretended not to hear.

Late that afternoon, Mrs. Cott took the car and drove into town to meet her husband when he finished work. They were going out to dinner and to the theater. Having an au pair girl certainly was giving his parents the chance to have a lot of good times, Lucas thought glumly. Here he was stuck at home.

"Be sure to shut all the windows if it rains," Mrs. Cott had instructed Lucas and Genevieve before she left. "It looks like we are going to have a storm."

The sky had been getting darker during the past hour, and from the distance they could hear the faint sound of thunder.

Genevieve was supervising Marcus and Marius on the swing set. The twins were no longer upset when their mother left them with their babysitter.

"Bye-bye," they called happily as they swung through the air.

Within ten minutes, the storm had moved closer. There was a streak of lightning followed by a loud clap of thunder and big drops of rain.

"Come. Inside the house," shouted Genevieve to the twins. "No more swinging."

"Rain. Rain," Marcus shouted. He jumped off his swing.

Marius jumped off his swing, too. "I like rain," he shouted as he tried to catch the drops of water in his hands.

Genevieve took the twins into the house. She and Lucas ran about, quickly shutting windows to prevent water from coming inside. The sky had gotten really dark now, and the rain was coming down very hard.

There was another streak of lightning, and it was immediately followed by a loud bang. "Did you hear that explosion?" shouted Lucas. "I bet it means trouble." He reached for the light switch, and as he had expected, nothing happened.

"Hey, Jennie. We've lost the electricity," he informed her.

"You mean there are no lights?" she asked him.

"Right," said Lucas, nodding. "No lights and no nothing." As he said it, he had a great idea. "If the electricity isn't working, the refrigerator won't be working, either," he informed Genevieve.

"Yes," she said, nodding her head. "It is the same at home."

"That means that the ice cream we bought this morning is going to melt inside the freezer."

Genevieve nodded her head. "It is too bad we bought such a large package," she said. "It will be a big waste."

"The best thing to do is eat it before it turns into a mush," said Lucas.

"It is too close to suppertime to eat ice cream," said Genevieve. Despite her foreign accent, she sounded just like his mother. It was the sort of thing a mother always said.

"It doesn't matter now," said Lucas. "We can't waste so much ice cream. My mother wouldn't want it all to go to waste," he said in his most convincing tone of voice.

"Yes," said Genevieve thoughtfully. "You are

right. Waste is not a good thing at all." She turned to the twins. "Come," she said. "We are all going to have ice cream."

In the kitchen, they lit a pair of candles to help them see better. Genevieve opened the freezer and removed the half-gallon of marshmallow fudge ripple ice cream. "It's still very cold," she told Lucas.

"It's cold now," Lucas replied. "But a power failure like this could last for hours. Maybe days." Once, when Lucas was about six years old, they had had a power failure that had lasted for almost twenty-four hours. However, he knew that most of the time when they lost electricity, it was restored within less than an hour. It was therefore very important that they hurry and begin eating the ice cream right now.

Genevieve went to the cupboard and got dishes for all of them.

"We had better eat as much as we can," said Lucas.

Marcus and Marius each ate a big helping of ice cream. Genevieve had two dishes. And the

one and only Lucas Cott managed to consume no fewer than three full dishes of marshmallow fudge ripple ice cream. He was just scraping up the last of his third dish when the lights came back on.

The kitchen clock said twenty minutes to five. However, Genevieve's wristwatch, which worked with a battery and did not stop when the electric power stopped, showed that it was really ten minutes to six.

"It is almost time for supper," Genevieve observed.

"I don't want any supper tonight," said Lucas. "This ice cream was my supper."

It was also, he thought, his third victory of the day.

"Oh no," said Genevieve. "You just had your dessert before your main course, that's all. It would be a shame to waste the good fresh string beans and fresh fish that we bought today."

The au pair girl smiled at Lucas. "When Marcus and Marius took their nap today, I watched a film on television. I learned a new American expression that you did not teach me."

"What is it?" asked Lucas.

"I wasn't *born yesterday*," said Genevieve. She smiled triumphantly at Lucas.

Lucas had not watched the movie with Genevieve. Still, he was pretty sure that he knew what the expression meant. It meant that he shouldn't expect to have victories over Jennie. She had his number.

LUCAS LEARNS TO DANCE

Although the summer was almost over and Genevieve spent most of every day with Marcus and Marius, she still could not tell the twins apart.

Lucas thought this was very funny. Genevieve, however, solved the problem. She called both little boys *moan Jerry*. It sounded strange to Lucas. Neither boy was named Jerry. His mother explained that Genevieve really was saying *mon cheri*.

"It means 'my dear' in French," said Mrs. Cott.

"They aren't hers and they aren't deers," protested Lucas. "She doesn't know which is which."

He was glad that he was smarter than Jennie about the twins. After all, they were his brothers and he'd been helping to take care of them long before she came on the scene. He was smarter than she was about other things, too. Genevieve still didn't know how to work the VCR or the electric can opener.

Nevertheless, although he had been prepared to dislike her, Lucas found himself enjoying Jennie more and more. At first, it was strange always to have a guest at every single meal. Still, with the passing weeks, she seemed more like a member of their family than a guest.

Hanging around home so much during the summer, he had begun to see what a tough job his mother had. He understood now why she had needed someone, in addition to himself, to be around to help take care of the twins. It seemed as if a day rarely passed without one twin or the other attempting to get into serious mischief. Looking back, Lucas felt bad about the day he had climbed the ladder to the roof. His mother needed to count on him to help her, not give her something else to worry about. So Lucas worked hard to regain his parents' trust.

Sometimes, in the evening when the twins were in bed for the night, Genevieve played cards with him. He was surprised that she knew some of the same games that he did. In fact, if it weren't for her funny pronunciation and her occasional errors when she spoke, you would think she was an American.

Jennie loved American music. In the afternoons, when the twins were napping, she often sat in the living room and listened to the radio. She didn't listen to the kind of slow, dreary music his parents did. She liked rock and roll. While she listened, she sang along with the singers. Even though the songs were in English, she knew all the words. Genevieve could sing and write letters home at the same time.

When she finished writing, Genevieve would

dance. Sometimes, Lucas watched her. Lucas always had thought that dancing was something you did with your feet. When Jennie danced, though, every part of her body seemed to move. She moved her head back and forth and, as her head moved, her long dark hair moved, too. Her hips swayed and her shoulders and arms also moved. Even her fingers moved in time to the music. Lucas watched with fascination.

One afternoon, when Lucas was peeking in the living-room door to watch Genevieve dance, she reached out and grabbed him by the arm.

"You dance, too," she said as she pulled him toward her.

"Naw," said Lucas, pulling away. "I can't dance."

"I will teach you," said Genevieve. "At home, all the boys dance. You will never have a girlfriend if you can't dance."

Lucas made a face. "I don't want a girlfriend," he said.

Genevieve laughed. "Not today," she said. "Not tomorrow. But someday you will. I know it for sure. You are a handsome boy. The girls will be crazy for you. But it will be much better if you can dance, too."

Lucas blushed and shook his head. "No way."

"Dancing is fun," said Genevieve. She took Lucas's hand. "Like this," she said. "Just do what I do."

It was a little like playing Simon Says with his brothers, Lucas decided. The only difference was that Jennie didn't speak. She stood opposite Lucas, shifting her weight from foot to foot. Then she raised an arm up into the air. "Lift your arm," she instructed Lucas.

He felt a little silly, but luckily no one was around to see him. Since he didn't have anything else to do until Julio came over to play, he guessed he could do this for a little while. Cautiously, Lucas moved his arm just the way Genevieve did.

"That's right," she said. "Do you feel the music?" She moved her other arm.

Lucas moved his other arm, too. He did everything Genevieve did. It was as if he was looking in a mirror. When she moved her right hip, he moved his left hip. When Genevieve moved her left hip, he moved his right one.

"Listen for the beat of the music," Genevieve said. She waved her arms and moved her hips at the same time. Lucas tried to copy her.

"You can do it," she said encouragingly. "The girls will be mad for you."

Lucas felt his face getting hot. Even though he was embarrassed by Genevieve's praise, he kept on dancing. It was sort of fun. It was almost like doing a kind of exercise. It was probably good for his muscles to dance like this, he told himself. He raised his arms over his head and stretched them in time to the music. Maybe his arms would grow faster if he did that. Then he would be better at shooting basketballs.

"Bravo, Lucas!" Genevieve called to him. She shook her head, and her long hair covered her face.

Lucas shook his head. For a fraction of a moment, he wished he had long hair, too.

"Hey, man. Look at you," a voice called out.

Lucas froze in his place. It was Julio's voice. His friend was standing in the doorway of the living room and grinning at Lucas. Lucas had not heard Julio arrive. Probably the music had drowned out the sound of the doorbell.

"I'm not dancing," Lucas said. "I was just doing some stretching exercises. Dancing is sissy stuff." He glared at Genevieve. How had she trapped him into doing this, anyhow?

"Come off it," said Julio, laughing. "I saw you dancing."

"You think I was dancing, but I wasn't," Lucas protested again. He wondered if he could ever live it down. He was furious at Genevieve. It was all her fault that Julio thought he was dancing.

Genevieve had not stopped dancing yet. She moved toward Julio and grabbed his hand. "Come. You dance, too," she said.

Lucas smiled. Now she was going to make Julio into a sissy, too, he thought.

Julio began to move to the music. He didn't

just copy Genevieve the way Lucas had been doing. He moved in a different way, turning around and covering more of the floor.

"Julio. You don't need any lessons from me." Genevieve laughed. "You are a pro."

Lucas stood watching in amazement. It was true. Julio was a better dancer than Genevieve.

"Let me try that," said Genevieve. She began to copy some of Julio's movements. "Where did you learn all this?" she asked.

"My big brothers taught me," said Julio proudly. "They're both good dancers."

That was news to Lucas. Julio was always telling about how his brother Nelson was on the soccer team at school. And his other brother Ramon was a super basketball player. Julio never talked about *dancing*.

"Hey, aren't we going to play? Don't you want to shoot baskets or something?" Lucas asked Julio.

"Later," said Julio. "Come on. Aren't you going to dance with us?"

So that was why, when Mrs. Cott walked into

the living room a few minutes later, she saw eighteen-year-old Genevieve Lamont dancing with the two young boys. She was surprised by what she saw. Lucas was surprised, too. He was surprised to be dancing, and he was surprised to be enjoying himself so much.

· 8 ·
AT THE MOVIES

Two more weeks and summer vacation would be over. Two more weeks and school would start again. How could the whole summer have gone so quickly? Lucas wondered.

In less than two more weeks, Genevieve would be gone. Lucas decided that he would miss her. It hadn't been bad having her around all summer. In fact, he wondered how he ever would have had a chance to play with Julio or any of his other friends if Genevieve hadn't been there to watch and distract the twins. How could he have shot any basketballs if Marcus and Marius were underfoot? It was absolutely impossible to play Monopoly or cards or build a jigsaw puzzle with his two little brothers grabbing at everything. Thank goodness for Genevieve!

On the next to the last Wednesday of summer vacation, Lucas woke to discover it was raining outside. Sometimes on rainy days this summer, he had gone to play at Julio's house. Once on a rainy day, Lucas's mother had taken Lucas and Julio to the science museum. Marcus and Marius had stayed home with Genevieve. Today, however, Julio had gone off somewhere with his brothers, and Mrs. Cott had a bad headache.

"I'm just not up to any trips today," she told Lucas when he asked if she would take him to the museum again.

"I'll teach you a new card game when the little ones are napping," Genevieve promised Lucas. She put them in their beds for their afternoon rest. These days, as the twins were nearing their third birthday, it was getting harder and harder to make them take that afternoon nap. Neither Marcus nor Marius wanted to sleep. They kept jumping out of bed and coming to see what Lucas was doing. Lucas wasn't doing much. He was feeling bored.

Lucas opened the newspaper to look at the comics. As he turned the pages, he found a big ad.

"There's a whole afternoon of cartoons at Movie World today," he reported to his mother. "It starts at two o'clock. Could I go?"

"Genevieve could drive you there," said Mrs. Cott. "Perhaps a short ride in the car would soothe the twins."

"I want to see the movies," shouted Marcus, who had overheard this exchange.

"Me, too!" shouted Marius, running from the bedroom. He didn't know what they were talking about but he didn't want to be left out of anything.

"You're too little to watch movies," said their mother.

"Genevieve and I could take care of them,"

offered Lucas. "They watch TV, so they could sit still at the movies, too," he suggested.

"Yes. Yes," said Marcus, jumping up and down. "Take me to the movies."

"I want to go, too," shouted Marius.

Mrs. Cott sighed. "All right." She gave in. "This will be an experiment and it will give me a little peace and quiet this afternoon."

"You need a piece of quiet," Genevieve agreed. "You'll be good, won't you?" she asked the twins.

"Yes," said Marcus.

"Me, too," said Marius.

At the movie theater, there was a huge number of children and parents. "I guess all the mothers wanted to have a piece of quiet this afternoon," said Genevieve. It was the second time she had made that mistake between *piece* and *peace*. This time, Lucas explained about *peace* and *piece*. In a way, those words were twins, like Marcus and Marius. They were the same and yet different.

Lucas looked around. He saw Cricket Kaufman standing on line to buy a ticket. She was with another girl, whom Lucas didn't know. He was surprised that Cricket liked cartoons. Lucas recognized many other kids from school. There were several kids who looked as young as his brothers.

Genevieve bought four tickets, and then they could enter. Inside the theater, the cartoons had not begun yet. The overhead lights were on so they could look for seats. There were so many children that they had to look around for a couple of minutes until they could find four seats together. Genevieve went in first, then Marcus and Marius. Lucas got the seat on the aisle. The twins were so small that their legs didn't reach the floor but stuck out on their seats instead.

"You must sit very quietly. Pretend you are watching television at home," he instructed his brothers. "You look with your eyes and not with your mouth," he added. He remembered that when he was little, his mother always had said that to him.

All around them, other children were rattling

candy papers and making a lot of noise. Marcus stood up on his seat to see better.

"You must sit down because no one can see behind you," said Genevieve.

"Where is the movie?" asked Marcus, looking around.

"It will begin very soon now," said Genevieve.

Sure enough, the lights dimmed and they were sitting in the darkened theater. Only the red lights above the exits were left on. Loud music began and the screen lit up.

"It's the movies!" shouted Marcus.

All the other children were talking, so it didn't seem important to remind him about looking with his eyes.

Once the action began on the screen, the audience quieted down. Lucas alternated watching the cartoons with glances at his brothers. They were both mesmerized by the huge screen in front of them. Marius had his thumb in his mouth. That was one of the ways that he differed from his twin, Lucas realized. Marcus never sucked his thumb, but sometimes when he was sitting quietly, Marius did.

Lucas reached over and tapped Genevieve on the shoulder. "Jennie, do we have enough money for popcorn?" he asked.

Genevieve nodded. She reached into her pocket and handed Lucas some money. "I'll watch the little ones," she said. "You get the popcorn."

There was no one on line for candy or popcorn now that the cartoons had begun, so Lucas returned quickly holding two containers of popcorn.

Lucas handed one of the containers of popcorn to Genevieve. He would share his popcorn with Marius, and Marcus could share with Genevieve. He had the better deal, since Marius had his thumb in his mouth. Lucas might not have to share at all.

The first cartoon ended and the children in the audience whistled and cheered. A second one began. Lucas sat back and enjoyed himself. The popcorn was hot and salty, just the way he liked it.

Lucas became absorbed in the cartoon. His eyes were on the screen and his hand automatically went from the popcorn container to his mouth. As the second cartoon came to an end, he looked over at the twins sitting between Genevieve and himself. He saw Marius sitting with his eyes glazed with half sleep. Somehow, though, incredibly, Marcus was not sitting on his seat.

Lucas leaned over to get a better look. Maybe Marcus had changed his seat and was now on the far side of Genevieve.

"Jennie. Where's my brother?" hissed Lucas.

The baby-sitter turned her head from the screen. She noticed the empty seat next to her and let out a gasp. "I don't know," she said. Her voice was full of fear.

Lucas felt sick. It could have been from eating the popcorn too fast, but he didn't think so.

How could they have lost Marcus? He was sure Marcus hadn't walked up or down the aisle. He would have seen him. Lucas looked down on the floor. Even in the half darkness, he could see bits of popcorn and candy wrappers all around. He noticed that there was a narrow space underneath each seat. It was big enough for a little boy or a small adult to crawl under.

"Maybe he's under here," he said to Genevieve. "I'll look for him."

Lucas got down on his hands and knees and looked under the seat where Marcus had been sitting. He put out his hand and tried to feel if his brother was underneath. He didn't feel anything, so he stuck his head under the seat and began to push himself forward, under first one seat and then another. As he went, he called out softly, "Marcus. Marcus, where are you?"

There were a lot of feet all around Lucas. Someone gave him a little kick in the head, but Lucas kept sliding forward. He had a feeling this was the direction in which the missing twin had gone.

"What are you doing under my seat?" a boy asked Lucas.

"I'm looking for my brother," he whispered.

"What would he be doing there? You can't see the movie from down there."

Lucas didn't bother to explain any further. He pushed himself forward and under the next seat. He grabbed hold of the bottom of the seat, and a woman's voice screamed out. Lucas let go fast. He realized that he had grabbed someone's leg.

"Help," the woman screamed again.

Lucas moved forward as fast as he could.

"Help!"

The action on the screen seemed a lot less interesting to the audience than the action in the theater. Some of the kids began calling out.

"I think it's a mouse or a rat," said the woman.

"I hate mice!" screamed another woman.

"Rats are worse," shouted another voice.

"Turn on the lights," another parent called out.

Lucas kept pushing forward. Marcus had to be here somewhere.

Then, even though he was on the floor beneath a seat, he could see that the lights had been turned on. Lucas tried to stand up, but he didn't

have enough room. He had to turn the angle of his body so he could slide out the other way. Finally, he reached the aisle.

Four rows back, where he had grabbed the woman by the leg, an usher was poking about with a broom.

"Has anyone seen the mouse?" the usher asked.

"No. But I felt him. He felt as big as a cat," someone said.

"He was as big as a dog," said someone else.

Lucas knew he was bigger than a cat or a dog, but he didn't have time to explain to everyone about it. He had to find Marcus. Now that the lights were on, he could look about better. He ran toward the front of the movie theater.

"Marcus," he shouted. There was so much commotion in the movie house that he no longer had to whisper and worry about disturbing anyone. "Marcus, where are you?"

"Lucas," a familiar voice called out.

It was Marcus, but Lucas didn't see him. He looked up and down the aisles.

"I got the best seat," called Marcus.

Lucas looked again. Sure enough, there was Marcus sitting in the very front row.

Lucas ran over to him. "How did you get here?" he asked. "You weren't supposed to leave the seat you already had."

"I dropped my popcorn," said Marcus.

"Everyone drops popcorn," said Lucas, remembering all the popcorn he had crawled over during his search for his brother.

"Mommy always says *pick up*," said Marcus.

It was true. Their mother always made the boys pick up the cookies or raisins or crayons that dropped on the floor at home.

"In the movies, no one picks up," said Lucas. "Besides, how did you get here?"

"I just got here," said Marcus.

Lucas guessed he had taken the same route under the seats that he had. Being smaller, it had been a lot easier for Marcus.

"Come on," said Lucas. "We've got to sit next to Genevieve and Marius."

He took his brother by his very sticky hand and

led him back toward the row where they had been sitting before.

Halfway up the aisle, he saw Genevieve coming toward him. "Look," she called. A huge smile of relief was on her face. "When the lights came on, I told Marius not to leave his seat. And I walked around and I found Marcus." She held up the twin's hand she was holding.

"That's Marius," said Lucas. "You found Marius and he wasn't even lost. *I* found Marcus."

Genevieve looked down and noticed for the first time that Lucas was holding a twin by the hand, too. Then she shrugged her shoulders. "A whole summer," she said, "and I never can tell them apart. I am so stupid."

"You're not stupid. You're very smart," Lucas insisted. "You've learned so much English this summer. You know hundreds of new words."

Genevieve smiled at Lucas. "You are a good boy, Lucas. You make me feel better." Then she turned to Marius. "Why did you get out of your seat?" she asked. "You promised you would stay."

"I forgot," said Marius.

"Everyone, back in your seats," the usher called out. By now, the aisles were filled with lots of boys and girls. "There's no mouse. We're going to turn the lights off again."

Lucas and Genevieve, each holding a twin by the hand, found their seats and sat down again. "You know what?" said Lucas to Genevieve. "We better each hold one of the boys by the hand for the rest of the movies." The popcorn was all gone, so he didn't need his hands for holding the container and eating. There were six more cartoons to go, and Lucas didn't want to risk losing either of his brothers or missing any of the movies, either.

"No sweat," said Genevieve. It was an expression she had picked up from Julio.

That was easy for her to say. She hadn't crawled on her hands and knees half the length of the movie house looking for Marcus. Lucas's stomach didn't bother him anymore, but he was damp with sweat. He kept holding on to Marcus's hand as he settled back to watch the cartoons.

The lights went off and the next cartoon started.

It sure wasn't easy taking care of the twins, Lucas thought. He had been scared when it seemed that Marcus was lost. It was just the way his mother felt when she saw him sitting up on the roof, Lucas realized. He hadn't been afraid to go up there, and Marcus hadn't been afraid sitting alone in the front seat of the auditorium, either. Still, both times, there had been the possibility of danger. He'd have to keep trying not to scare his mother again. He also would have to do a better job of setting a good example for the twins. He was the only big brother they had, and they liked to copy everything that he did.

Lucas looked over to be sure that Marius was safe in his seat next to Genevieve. Then, reassured that all was well, he sat back in his seat and focused his attention on the screen. He squeezed Marcus's hand gently. Pretty soon, the twins would be old enough to play real games with him. They were lucky to have him for a brother, he realized. Too bad there was only one of him to go around. After all, he had two of them. He'd just have to work twice as hard at being a good big brother. He knew he could do it.

· 9 ·
AU REVOIR, GENEVIEVE

Mrs. Cott took Lucas shopping for back-to-school clothes.

"How could we have gone to all these stores without Genevieve?" she asked Lucas.

New clothing, especially clothes to wear to school, was not important to Lucas, so he didn't wonder how they could have managed a shopping trip if they didn't have Genevieve to watch Marcus and Marius.

On the other hand, he did wonder how it would feel when she was gone. Two more days and Genevieve would be flying home to France. Four more days and Lucas would be beginning fourth grade.

"This has been a wonderful summer for me," said Mrs. Cott to Lucas. "But I think it wasn't as good as it could have been for you."

"It was great," Lucas protested. "Summer's the best season of the year. I just wish it lasted longer," he added.

"Summer is a wonderful time of year," said Mrs. Cott. "But I think next summer it will be even better for you. Your father and I have been discussing sending you to sleep-away camp for a few weeks next year. What do you think of that?"

"Sleep-away camp?" said Lucas with surprise. He thought of all the things he had heard kids at school say about summer camps. It sounded as if it might be loads of fun. In fact, he wished it was next summer already.

"Will Genevieve come back here next year?"

asked Lucas. If he was away at camp, he would miss seeing her.

"No," said Mrs. Cott. "Next year, Genevieve wants to spend some time in England."

"Oh," said Lucas.

"Perhaps she will be able to come and visit with us again some other time," said Mrs. Cott. "I'm going to miss her."

"Me, too," Lucas said.

The whole family was going to miss the au pair girl. She had become a regular part of their household.

The day before Genevieve left, Mrs. Cott wanted to prepare a special meal. "Oh no," Genevieve protested. "Please let me cook the food for this evening. I want to make a real French dinner for you. It will give me much pleasure."

So Lucas and his mother took the twins off to a local playground for the afternoon and Genevieve stayed home to cook. Lucas wondered what kind of food Genevieve would cook for this French meal. Luckily, they didn't sell horsemeat around here. He had heard that French people ate other weird things like snails and frogs, though. He didn't remember seeing those items for sale at the supermarket, either. What would Genevieve cook?

The farewell dinner was delicious. First, there was something called pâté. It tasted a bit like liverwurst. It was made in France, and Genevieve had brought a small can of it from home in her luggage.

"I was planning to give it to you all summer," she said, beaming.

Next, there was a casserole with meat cut up in little pieces with mushrooms and onions and gravy. Lucas wondered briefly if it could be horse-meat, after all. He was relieved when Genevieve announced that they were eating boeuf Bour-guignon. She pronounced it differently from the way he did, but he knew he was chewing good old American beef. Once he knew what he was eating, Lucas thought it tasted fine.

There was salad with mustard in the dressing.

"It's French Dijon mustard, of course," said Genevieve.

Lucas thought mustard belonged on hot dogs and not in salad, but he was polite and ate a small portion. Even the twins were behaving very well for boys of their age. They didn't spill any of their food, and they kept busy chewing on pieces of the crusty French bread that Genevieve had been able to buy in town.

Of course, the best part of the meal was the dessert. It looked like a big peach pie to Lucas. Genevieve insisted it was a *tarte*. Lucas didn't care what you called it. It was good.

"Now I am going to make a speech," announced Genevieve as the meal came to an end.

"A speech?" said Mr. Cott with surprise.

"Yes. I have written a special speech," said Genevieve. She reached into the pocket of the skirt she was wearing and pulled out a folded piece of paper. She opened the paper and looked around the table. "I am going to try and use some of the new expressions that you all taught me this summer. My notebook is almost full, and my head is full, too," she said. Then she cleared her throat and began reading.

"It is nothing to sneeze at to travel so many miles and live with another family," she began.

"When I got on the airplane in Paris, I was in a stew. I had cold feet. First I felt blue. Then I felt chicken. But I tried to be brave. I knew it would not be a piece of cake to take care of twin brothers. Perhaps I would get fired before the summer was over. Luckily, I had the help of Lucas.

"I discovered that Lucas likes to horse around and to pull my leg. At first, he bugged me. But Lucas was a big help. When it was raining cats and dogs, Lucas played with his brothers so they would not get bored. He also helped me with my English.

"Now I am going home. I am going to miss you all. I hope someday you will come to France to visit me. Au revoir."

Lucas's mother got up from her place and hugged Genevieve. "We are all going to miss you, too," she said, wiping tears from her eyes.

Lucas turned to his brothers. "We have a surprise for Genevieve," he said. "Are you ready?" he asked Marcus and Marius. Lucas had been coaching them for the past week. It was not easy to find time when Genevieve was not around. Nor was it easy for boys as young as Marcus and Marius to keep a secret. Somehow they had managed. Now they could show off to everyone.

"One-two-three-go," said Lucas. The twins began singing.

"*Frère Jacques, Frère Jacques. Dormez-vous?*"

"They are singing in French," Genevieve squealed with delight.

Lucas's parents knew he had been teaching the song to the boys, but they were surprised, too, at how well they performed.

When Marcus and Marius sang the final words of the song, Genevieve got out of her seat and ran and gave them each a kiss. Then she turned and put her arms around Lucas. "You are a wonderful brother to the little boys. And I think you are like a brother to me, too," she said. She gave Lucas a big kiss on each cheek.

Lucas's face turned bright red. Somehow, though, he didn't really mind being kissed by Genevieve. He knew that he was going to miss her a lot. It was another of those surprises that didn't come in a box. Sometimes they could be a lot better than you expected.